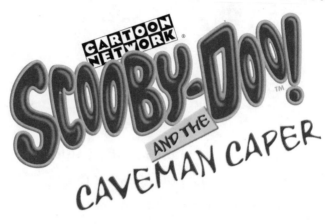

Look for the **Scooby-Doo Mysteries**.
Collect them all!

Written by
James Gelsey

A
LITTLE APPLE
PAPERBACK

SCHOLASTIC INC.

New York Toronto London Auckland Sydney
Mexico City New Delhi Hong Kong Buenos Aires

If you purchased this book without a cover, you should be aware that this book is stolen property. It was reported as "unsold and destroyed" to the publisher, and neither the author nor the publisher has received any payment for this "stripped book."

No part of this publication may be reproduced in whole or in part, or stored in a retrieval system, or transmitted in any form or by any means, electronic, mechanical, photocopying, recording, or otherwise, without written permission of the publisher. For information regarding permission, write to Scholastic Inc., Attention: Permissions Department, 555 Broadway, New York, NY 10012.

ISBN 0-439-24238-X

Copyright © 2001 by Hanna-Barbera.
SCOOBY-DOO and all related characters and elements
are trademarks of and © Hanna-Barbera.
CARTOON NETWORK and logo are trademarks of
and © Cartoon Network.
(s01)
Published by Scholastic Inc. All rights reserved.
SCHOLASTIC, LITTLE APPLE PAPERBACKS, and associated logos are
trademarks and/or registered trademarks of Scholastic Inc.

Designed by Carisa Swenson

12 11 10 9 8 7 6 5 4 3 2 1   1 2 3 4 5 6/0

Special thanks to Duendes del Sur for cover and interior illustrations.
Printed in the U.S.A.
First Scholastic printing, September 2001

For Michelle and Ed

Chapter 1

"Hey, who drank all of my hot cocoa?" Shaggy called from the back of the Mystery Machine.

"What hot cocoa?" Velma asked.

"Like, the hot cocoa I was bringing to the ice rink so I could stay warm," Shaggy replied. "Did you drink it, Fred?"

"I've been driving the whole time, Shaggy," Fred answered.

"How about you, Daphne?" Shaggy interrogated her. "You look like you've gotten a little warmer since we left the malt shop."

"That's because I'm wearing my ice-skating outfit," Daphne said.

"And don't look at me," Velma said. "I don't like hot cocoa."

That left only one other suspect. Shaggy turned and looked at Scooby, who whistled as he looked out the rear window of the van.

"Scooby-Doo?" Shaggy asked suspiciously.

"Ruh?" Scooby answered innocently.

"Did you drink my hot cocoa?" Shaggy asked.

Scooby turned around, shaking his head.

"Ruh-uh," he barked.

Fred looked into the rearview mirror and started laughing. Daphne and Velma turned around and began laughing, too.

"Rat's ro runny?" asked Scooby.

"Like, Scoob, either you're a bad liar or you've grown a chocolate beard and mustache," Shaggy said with a smile.

Scooby crossed his eyes so he could look down at his whiskers. He licked his tongue across his entire mouth and slurped in the rest of the hot cocoa.

"Ree-hee-hee-hee-hee-hee," he giggled.

"Don't worry, Shaggy," Velma said. "I'm sure there's going to be plenty of hot cocoa at the arena."

"But remember, we're not going to the rink to drink hot cocoa," Fred said. "We're going so that Daphne can skate with Betty Kunkle."

Shaggy and Scooby laughed when they heard her name.

"Like, who's Betty Kunkle?" asked Shaggy, giggling as he said her name.

"She used to be one of the top professional

figure skaters," Daphne explained. "She won a gold medal at the last Olympics. But then she decided to start her own ice-skating show, which is why she's here. The very first performance of 'Betty Kunkle's Silver Skates Arctic Ice Revue' is going to be tonight."

"Then why are we going there in the middle of the afternoon?" Shaggy asked.

"Because Daphne won that ice-skating contest at the mall, remember?" Velma said. "The grand prize was a chance to skate with Betty Kunkle."

Shaggy laughed again.

"What's so funny?" Daphne asked.

"I don't know, Daphne," Shaggy said. "I guess it's that name. Every time I hear it, it makes me want to laugh."

"Well, you'd better figure out how to control

yourself," she warned. "I don't want you embarrassing us when we meet her."

"Reet roo?" Scooby asked.

"Betty Kunkle," Daphne answered.

Scooby started giggling, but Shaggy tried to hold it in. After a moment, he couldn't take it anymore. He exploded into laughter. Shaggy and Scooby rolled on the floor in the back of the van.

"Oh, brother," Velma sighed.

"All right, you two, that's enough," Fred said. "We're pulling into the arena. Remember what Daphne said. Don't do anything that will embarrass us."

"I know, like laughing at Betty What's-her-name's name," Shaggy said.

"Or causing any trouble," Daphne added.

"What kind of trouble could we cause at an ice arena?" asked Shaggy.

"We don't know, and we don't want to find out!" Velma answered.

Chapter 2

As Fred parked the van, Daphne took a piece of paper out of her pocket and read it.

"According to this letter, we're supposed to use the stage entrance in the back," she said.

"Then let's go, gang," Fred said, leading everyone around the building to the back. They found the stage entrance and knocked on the big metal door. The knock seemed to echo through the building. A moment later, the door opened and a stocky bald man in a rumpled blue suit came out. He wore a gray tie, black earmuffs, and work boots.

"Can I help you kids?" he asked.

"Hi, I'm Daphne Blake," Daphne said. "And this is Fred, Velma, Shaggy, and Scooby-Doo."

The man looked at the gang without blinking. "Can I help you kids?" he asked again.

"I'm the winner of the Shoppingland Mall contest," Daphne explained, handing him the letter. "I'm here to skate with Betty Kunkle."

Shaggy and Scooby looked at each other and tried with all their might not to laugh out loud.

The man read the letter. "Shoppingland, Shoppingland," he muttered to himself. "Never heard of it. If you want to see Betty Kunkle, buy some tickets."

Just as the man walked back inside, he bumped into a woman in a long overcoat. The woman whispered something into the man's ear. The man suddenly perked up. He turned and smiled at the gang.

"Shoppingland? Why didn't you say so?" he said. "So which one of you is the lucky winner?"

"I'd say she's the one wearing the skating outfit," the woman said. "Hi, I'm Raye Cleveland, Betty's coach. And you must be Daphne."

"Yes, that's me," Daphne replied.

"And I'm G. T. Barrington, Betty's publicist," the rumpled man said. "I'm the one who arranged the skating contest at the mall."

"It's G. T.'s job to whip up any kind of publicity he can," Raye explained. "And he'll stop at nothing to sell tickets."

"That's right," G. T. said. "If I didn't do my job, no one would be buying tickets to this thing. I may do strange things, but no one complains when we fill every seat."

"What kind of strange things?" Daphne asked.

"G. T. came up with the gimmick of Betty wearing ice skates with sterling silver blades."

"So that's why it's the 'Silver Skates Arctic Ice Revue,'" Daphne said.

"That's right," G. T. said proudly. "I gave Betty a pair of silver ice skates and now that's all she'll wear. She won't skate in anything else. But that's not all. I paid a guy up in Alaska to go to the Arctic and carve out some ice. He put it in a refrigerated truck and sent it down here. We put some of it out on the rink. That way, 'Betty Kunkle's Silver Skates Arctic Ice Revue' can boast real Arctic ice."

"You mean the ice in the rink is really from the Arctic?" asked Velma.

"You bet," G. T. answered with a broad smile. "And speaking of ice, I want to make sure my luxury box is stocked with refreshments. I have a lot of important people coming to the show later." G. T. headed back inside.

"Mr. Barrington mentioned that he put

some of the ice on the rink," Velma said. "What about the rest of it?"

"There was something strange inside one of the blocks," Raye said. "We called the university, and they said to keep it frozen until they could get here."

"What was it?" asked Fred.

"We're not sure, but it looked like a prehistoric caveman," Raye said. "I guess that ice has been around for centuries."

"Jinkies! A real, live caveman?" exclaimed Velma. "Do you think we could see it?"

"We'll pass it on the way in," Raye said. "So what do you say we go inside and meet Betty Kunkle?"

Shaggy and Scooby held in their laughter long enough for Fred, Daphne, and Velma to follow Raye inside. Then they cracked up.

"Let's go, you two," Velma said, poking her head out the door. She smiled at them.

11

Chapter 3

The gang followed Raye Cleveland into the building. They found themselves walking down a chilly hallway with pipes running along the ceiling.

"Right now, we're underneath the refrigeration units for the ice rink," Raye said. "And right over there is the freezer. That's where the caveman is."

"It looks like someone forgot to close the door," Fred said.

Raye opened the freezer door the rest of the way. She flipped on the light and looked around inside. Standing in the middle of the freezer was a huge block of ice with something frozen inside.

"It sure looks like a caveman, all right," Velma said.

The caveman seemed to be holding a large wooden club in one hand.

"Man, if that's not the creepiest thing I've ever seen, I don't know what is," Shaggy remarked. "Remind me to order my sodas without ice from now on."

"I'm glad you saw that open door, Fred," Raye said. "If too much warm air gets inside, that thing will start melting." She closed the door tightly and led the gang up a staircase at the end of the hallway.

A gigantic polar bear greeted them at the top of the stairs.

"Rikes!" Scooby barked, jumping into Shaggy's arms.

"Relax, Scooby, it's just a fake polar bear," Velma said.

"It's one of the set pieces for the show," Raye said. "I'd better have someone move it away from the stairs." She looked around and called out someone's name. "Phyllis? Phyllis?"

"Is this where all the sets for the show are kept?" Daphne asked.

"Yup," Raye answered. "Come on."

The gang followed Raye into an enormous space. It was chock-full of different pieces of scenery and props, all reflecting the ice show's Arctic theme. There was a pile of snow that turned out to be three lumpy white blankets, and lots of snowflakes made of plastic.

"Why is it so cold up here?" Shaggy asked, his teeth starting to chatter.

"If we made it any warmer, we'd have a bit of a flood on our hands. Look," Raye said. She walked over to a black curtain and pulled it aside. The gang looked through and saw the arena.

"There's the ice rink!" Daphne exclaimed. "It's right here!"

"That's right," Raye said. "This curtain is how the skaters and the sets get onto the ice."

As the gang peered out onto the ice, they suddenly heard a loud machine roar to life.

VRRRRRRRUUUUMMMMMMM!

"What was that?" asked Fred.

"That," Raye answered, "must be my sister, Phyllis. I pulled some strings and got her a job helping out around the show."

"I think your sister must have a sore throat or something," Shaggy said. "She sounds terrible."

"No, it's just Phyllis riding on the Zamboni," Raye said.

"You mean your sister's riding on top of an Italian dessert?" Shaggy asked.

"Shaggy, a Zamboni is a machine they use to clean and resurface the ice," Velma explained. "It was invented by a man named Zamboni. Raye's sister must be driving it."

"Exactly," Raye confirmed. Everyone looked out onto the ice and saw Phyllis steer the Zamboni machine out of its storage area next to the rink. Raye gave a whistle and motioned for Phyllis to come over.

Phyllis drove the Zamboni machine slowly across the ice. When she reached the gang, she shut off the engine and climbed down. She was wearing a big green parka, earmuffs, a red scarf around her neck, and heavy-duty work boots with thick treads.

"Phyl, Daphne here won the skating contest and gets to skate with Betty during her warm-ups," said Raye.

"You are so lucky," Phyllis gasped. "I would give anything to skate with Betty. I'm a professional skater myself, you know."

Raye cleared her throat and gave her sister a disbelieving look.

"All right, I *want* to be a professional skater," Phyllis said. "But I would do anything for a chance to be in a real ice show."

"Listen, Phyl, could you move that polar bear away from the stairs?" Raye asked. "Daphne, before I bring you to Betty, I just want to remind you to be careful skating with her."

"Of course I'll be careful," said Daphne. "Why do you say that?"

"Because Raye wouldn't want you to get in Betty's way by accident and cause her to fall or anything," Phyllis said. "Then she might not be able to skate and they'd have to find someone else to fill in. But *where* could they possibly find someone on such short notice who knows all the routines from watching Betty practice them for a week?" Phyllis asked, pretending to be puzzled.

"Phyl, just move the polar bear, please," Raye reminded her, sighing.

As Phyllis walked away, Raye turned back to the gang. "Don't mind Phyllis," Raye said. "She has this dream of filling in for an injured skater and being 'discovered.' Anyway, let's go. I'm sure Betty can't wait to meet you!"

Chapter 4

Raye started leading the gang away when they heard someone scream.

"Aaaaaagh!"

Everyone turned and saw a man push Phyllis and the stuffed polar bear out of the way.

"You scared the daylights out of me!" the man yelled.

"Sorry," Phyllis said, carrying the polar bear away.

The man saw Raye and zoomed right over. He was wearing a red sweater over a black turtleneck and black pants.

"Where is she, Raye?" the man asked.

"How did you get in here?" Raye shot back.

"Someone left the back door open," the man answered. "Now where's Betty?"

"She's busy getting ready for the show," Raye answered.

The man suddenly noticed that Daphne was staring at him.

"Yes, miss, can I help you?" he asked her.

"You're Joe Kresgee!" she said. "You're Betty's skating partner."

"I *was* Betty's skating partner," Joe Kresgee answered. "Until she decided to retire from competition without telling me, that is."

"Now don't blame Betty because your career fell apart," Raye said. "She's the reason you made it to the Olympics in the first place, so you should be grateful to her."

Joe Kresgee's face turned red with anger. Then he took a deep breath and calmly blinked his eyes.

"Of course, Raye," Joe said. "Would you please be so kind as to deliver a message for me to Ms. Kunkle?"

Shaggy let a small giggle escape. Joe Kresgee glared at him.

"Please tell Betty that I haven't forgiven her," he said. "And that she will pay dearly for ruining my ice-skating career. Did you get all that?"

Joe Kresgee whipped around and marched back downstairs.

"Wow, he's sure mad at Betty," Velma said.

"I think he's more jealous than anything," Raye said. "Now let's go meet her before anything else can distract us."

The gang followed Raye across the back-stage area and through a door. The door opened onto a short hallway with three other doors. Scooby's nose started twitching as he sniffed the air.

"What is it, pal?" asked Shaggy.

"Rot rocoa," Scooby said.

"I'll bet Betty's making some," Raye said. She walked up to the door with a silver star on it. "This is Betty's dressing room." She gave a special knock and the door opened. A woman dressed in a white-and-gold skating outfit stood in the doorway.

"What's up, Raye?" she asked.

"Betty, I'd like you to meet your skating partner for this afternoon's warm-ups," Raye said. "Daphne Blake, meet Betty Kunkle. Now please excuse me while I go check the ice."

Daphne smiled and stepped forward.

"It's so great to meet you, Ms. Kunkle," Daphne said. "I'm a big fan."

"Well, it's nice to meet you, too, Daphne," Betty replied. "Are these your friends?"

"Oh, yes," Daphne said. "This is Fred, Velma, Shaggy, and Scooby-Doo. I hope it's okay that I brought them."

"Of course," Betty said. "Why don't you all come inside for some hot cocoa?"

"We thought you'd never ask!" Shaggy said.

Chapter 5

Shaggy and Scooby barged right into Betty Kunkle's dressing room. They spied a sofa in the corner and flopped themselves down on it.

"Now this is more like it," Shaggy said. "Warm and comfy."

Fred noticed a pair of ice skates hanging on a hook.

"Are those your silver skates, Ms. Kunkle?" he asked.

"That's right," she replied. "G. T. Barrington gave them to me. I thought they were silly at first, but now I wouldn't dream of skating without them. Aren't they beautiful?"

"If they're silver, they must be very valuable," Velma said.

Suddenly, there was a loud growling sound outside Betty's dressing room door.

"Wh-wh-wh-what's that?" Shaggy cried.

"Maybe it's the polar bear," Daphne joked.

The door flew open.

"Or m-m-m-maybe it's the c-c-c-caveman!" Shaggy yelled.

"Rikes!" Scooby dove behind the sofa. Shaggy quickly followed.

The caveman burst into the room. He let out a fierce roar. Fred, Daphne, Velma, and Betty all backed away to the far side of the room. The caveman looked around the dressing room. Then he walked over to the wall, reached up, and grabbed the silver ice skates. He roared again and ran out of the room.

"Jinkies!" Velma exclaimed. "The caveman came back to life."

A moment later, Raye ran into the dressing room. "Betty! Are you all right?" she called.

"I'm fine, Raye," she replied. "Did you see it?"

"I saw it, all right," Raye said. "But I don't believe it. He knocked me over as he ran by me. I think he ran out onto the ice."

"Go tell G. T. that unless you find that caveman and get my silver skates back, you'll have to do the show without me," Betty demanded.

"But, Betty, without you there isn't any

show," Raye said pleadingly.

"We'd hate for you not to do the show," Daphne said. "There are so many people who are looking forward to seeing you."

"I have an idea," Fred offered. "Give us a chance to solve this mystery."

Raye thought for a moment and then nodded. "You're on, kids," she said. "The box office opens in two hours. You have until then to find that caveman and get back Betty's silver skates."

"Then let's not waste any time," Fred said. "Daphne and I will go after the caveman."

"And Shaggy, Scooby, and I will start investigating around here," Velma said.

"Let's meet backstage as soon as we find anything," Daphne said. She and Fred left the dressing room.

"Well, I certainly don't feel too safe staying here," Betty said. "That caveman may come back for more."

"Come with me, Betty," Raye said. "We'll go up to G. T.'s luxury box until this thing blows over."

Once Betty and Raye had gone, Velma looked around the room and then at the floor. Something caught her eye. She walked over to the doorway and glanced down the length of the hallway floor.

"That caveman knew exactly where he was going and exactly what he was looking for," Velma remarked.

"Like, how do you know that?" asked Shaggy.

"Because he left a trail of wet footprints behind," Velma said.

Shaggy and Scooby looked at the floor. "Those don't look like footprints," Shaggy said. "They look more like boot prints to me."

"Exactly, Shaggy," Velma said. "And they go in a straight line from the hallway, into the dressing room, right to the wall where the silver skates were hanging."

"But why would a caveman be wearing boots?" asked Shaggy.

"I'm glad you asked, Shaggy," Velma said. "Because that's what we're going to find out next."

"Me and my big mouth," Shaggy moaned.

Chapter 6

"Uh, Velma, you go ahead," Shaggy said. "Scooby and I want to have some of the hot cocoa that Betty offered us before tall, dark, and frozen burst in."

"I don't know . . ." Velma replied warily.

"Rease?" begged Scooby.

"We'll be really quick," Shaggy said. "Besides, all we have to do is follow those watery boot prints to find you."

"All right, but don't take too long," Velma warned them.

Velma left the dressing room. Shaggy and

Scooby ran over to the pot of hot cocoa. Shaggy grabbed two mugs and set them down next to the pot. He put a plastic spoon into each mug. Then he carefully poured the hot cocoa into each mug. He and Scooby picked up their mugs and slowly took a sip.

"Mmmmmmm," they said simultaneously, tasting the chocolaty goodness.

"Let's go, Scooby-Doo," Shaggy said. "We'll drink and walk."

Shaggy looked down and noticed that the boot prints were almost gone. "Oh, no!" he exclaimed. "The wet boot prints are drying up! Come on, Scoob. And hurry!"

Shaggy and Scooby walked as quickly as they could without spilling their hot cocoa.

They went into the hallway and through the doorway that led back to the big backstage area. They looked around, but there were no more boot prints. After another sip of cocoa, they heard a sound come from the far side of the room.

"Velma?" Shaggy called.

"Relma?" echoed Scooby.

They took a few steps in one direction. Then they heard another sound, this time closer. Shaggy turned around.

"Zoinks!" he exclaimed. He was standing face-to-face with a giant walrus. "Oh, it's just another prop for the ice show."

Scooby looked at the walrus and got an idea. He grabbed the plastic spoons from his and Shaggy's mugs of hot cocoa. Scooby turned around, raised the spoons to his face, and stood up on his hind legs. When Scooby turned back around, he brought his front legs together like flippers. The plastic spoons stuck out of his mouth like two walrus tusks. He banged his flipper paws together.

"Arrooooooooo, arrooooooo," he called.

"Hey, it's a Scooby walrus!" Shaggy laughed. "That's really good, pal. What other Arctic creatures can you do?"

Scooby looked at Shaggy. Then his eyes opened up wide and the spoons fell out of his mouth.

"R-r-r-raveman!" Scooby barked.

"You're going to imitate a caveman? Cool!" said Shaggy.

"Ruh-uh!" Scooby said, pointing over Shaggy's shoulder. "Raveman!"

Shaggy turned and saw the caveman standing there. The

caveman raised his wooden club and let out a loud yell.

"Let's get out of here!" Shaggy yelled.

He and Scooby weaved in and out of the pieces of scenery, with the caveman close behind them.

"This way, Scooby," Shaggy called. He and Scooby ran through the black curtain and onto the ice. They immediately lost control and started slipping and sliding. The caveman ran out onto the ice after them. Instead of slipping and sliding like Shaggy and Scooby, he was able to keep his footing.

Scooby managed to pick himself up and start running. Shaggy grabbed onto Scooby's tail and slid along the ice behind him. Just as the caveman was about to grab them, Scooby crashed into the side of the rink. The caveman leaped over Shaggy, Scooby, and the railing and ran off into the stands.

"Boy, that was close," Shaggy said. He and Scooby made their way across the ice back to the black curtain, holding on to the side of the rink the entire way. Velma was there waiting for them, and she was holding something in her hand.

"I was on my way downstairs when I heard your voices out on the ice," she said.

"You didn't happen to find our mugs of hot cocoa back here, did you?" asked Shaggy. "We sure could use them now."

"No, but I did find another clue," Velma said. She showed them a red thread. "I found it caught on the back of the walrus."

"That's where the caveman was hiding, all right," Shaggy said. "But what does that clue mean?"

"It means we need to find Fred and Daphne," Velma said. "We're close to solving this mystery, and I have a hunch they'll find the most important clue yet. Come on."

Chapter 7

Velma led Shaggy and Scooby down a flight of stairs and into the hallway.

"Hey, isn't this where the freezer is?" asked Shaggy.

"Right you are," Fred said, coming down the hall toward them. "This is where everything began."

"Fred and I just got here," Daphne explained. "After we left the dressing room, we followed some wet bootprints."

"We saw those, too," Velma said.

"We followed them to the entrance to the

ice rink," Fred continued. "But after looking around the rink, we couldn't find anything else."

"That's when we decided to examine where the caveman came from instead of trying to figure out where he went," Daphne concluded.

"Like, Scooby and I can tell you where he went," Shaggy said. "After us!"

Velma explained how the caveman chased Shaggy and Scooby across the ice and then disappeared. She also showed Fred and Daphne the red string she'd found.

"So I guess our last hope to find anything is here," Fred said. "In the freezer."

They opened the freezer door and turned on the lights. The huge slab of ice was gone. In its place, shards of broken ice were scattered all over the floor.

"It looks like the caveman shattered the ice to get out," Fred said. "Let's go take a closer look and see what we can find."

They all stepped into the freezer to look around. Just then, they heard a familiar growl come from the hallway.

"Man, I sure hope that's one of those prop polar bears," Shaggy whimpered.

The gang turned around and saw the caveman standing there. He waved his club at them and roared loudly. Then he stepped back and slammed the freezer door shut. The gang was trapped!

"NO! Wait!" Fred shouted. He ran over and pounded on the door. The caveman peered through the tiny window, waved, then disappeared.

"I c-c-c-can't believe we're locked in a freezer," moaned Shaggy. "I'm too young to become a Shagsicle."

"No one's going to become a frozen dessert, Shaggy," Velma said. "These doors are always made with an emergency release mechanism." She examined the door and found a curved handle at the end of a short metal rod. She leaned against the handle, but it didn't budge.

"It must be frozen," Velma said.

"Everyone needs to pitch in," Fred said. "I'll lean against the handle. Everyone else

line up behind me and push on the count of three."

Fred stood behind the handle. Daphne stood behind Fred, Velma behind Daphne, Shaggy behind Velma, and Scooby-Doo behind Shaggy.

"Ready? One. Two. Three!" Fred called.

Everyone leaned forward, pushing Fred against the emergency release handle. The metal rod moved slowly, and soon they heard a click. The freezer door was open.

The gang piled out of the freezer and warmed up in the hallway.

"Whew! Just in time," Shaggy said. "I think I was getting frostbite."

"That caveman sure gets around," Velma said.

"I'll say," Fred agreed. "It's like he's got wheels or something."

"If he's got wheels, he sure can't drive them," Daphne added, holding up a key.

"Look what I found in the freezer."

"Great clue, Daphne," Velma said. "I think it's time to turn up the heat on our Arctic caveman."

"Velma's right," Fred said. "Gang, it's time to set a trap!"

Chapter 8

"Here's the plan, gang, so listen up," Fred instructed. "The caveman must have known that Betty wouldn't perform without her silver skates. So if we're going to get him to come out, we need to convince him that Betty's going to skate as scheduled."

"And how are we going to do that?" Shaggy asked.

Fred, Daphne, and Velma looked at Shaggy and smiled.

"When am I going to learn to keep my big mouth shut?" sighed Shaggy.

"It's very simple, Shaggy," Fred explained. "Scooby-Doo will dress up like Betty and pretend to warm up. You'll pretend to be Betty's coach. Once the caveman sees you on the ice, he's bound to come out. Velma, Daphne, and I will be hiding behind the railing. When the caveman comes out, lure him over to the side. We'll jump up and capture him in one of the snow blankets."

"You're right, Fred, it sounds simple," Shaggy said. "Too bad it won't work."

"Why not?" asked Fred.

"Because Scooby and I are on a cold strike," Shaggy answered. "We're not doing anything until it gets a little warmer in here."

They looked over and saw Scooby rubbing his paws together, trying to get warm.

"Come on, Scooby," Daphne said. "It's only a few more minutes. Then we'll go outside and warm up. We promise."

"Ruh-uh," Scooby said, shaking his head.

"Will you do it for a thermos of hot cocoa?" offered Velma.

"Rope," Scooby said.

"Will you do it for a thermos of hot cocoa and a Scooby Snack?" tried Daphne.

Scooby thought for exactly one second.

"Rokay!" he barked. He sat up, waiting for Daphne to toss his Scooby Snack to him. She did, and he gobbled it down in a single gulp.

"Daphne, you take Shaggy and Scooby to get ready," Fred said. "Velma and I will find a snow blanket and get into position."

Daphne took Shaggy and Scooby to Betty's dressing room. Shaggy put on a big overcoat, while Scooby put on one of Betty's skating outfits. Daphne laced her skates onto Scooby's rear paws. Then she helped him walk over to the ice rink.

"All you have to do is lean forward slightly and take turns pushing off with each leg," Daphne said. "Good luck, Scooby."

She gave him a soft push onto the ice. Shaggy followed him and tried not to make any sudden moves. Scooby flailed his arms about until he could regain his balance. Then he carefully leaned forward a bit and pushed off with his right leg. He slowly but steadily sailed across the ice.

"Good job, Scooby-Doo, uh, I mean, Betty," Shaggy called. "Why don't you try that move

again? It'll be wonderful in the show tonight, since you've definitely decided to skate."

Scooby became more comfortable and slowly picked up speed. He skated around and around until he and Shaggy heard the caveman's roar echo through the arena.

"Rikes!" Scooby barked, losing his balance. Shaggy saw the caveman come running down through the stands. The caveman leaped over the railing and landed on the ice without falling.

"AAARRRRRRGGGGHHHH!" growled the caveman.

"Let's get moving, Scooby!" Shaggy called.

He tried to run over to help Scooby, but he slipped and fell down. Scooby tried to scramble to his feet but kept slipping, too. The caveman was getting closer. Finally, Scooby and Shaggy managed to get to their feet. Scooby leaned forward and pushed off with his right leg. Shaggy held on as they skated toward the railing with the caveman right behind them.

Just as Scooby neared the railing, Shaggy yelled, "Now, Fred!"

Fred and Velma jumped up and threw the snow blanket. The caveman saw it coming but couldn't stop in time. The blanket landed squarely on him and Shaggy, knocking them to the ice.

"Over here, Scooby!" Daphne said, waving to Scooby. Scooby skated over to Daphne, who tossed him the key they'd found. Scooby grabbed the key and skated over to a green door.

Shaggy squirmed under the blanket so much that it came off the caveman. The caveman got up and started running around the rink, looking for Scooby. Suddenly, he heard the sound of a motor starting.

VRRRRRRRUUUUMMMMMMM!

Scooby drove the Zamboni machine onto the ice. The caveman roared and tried to run away. Scooby steered the Zamboni all over the rink, chasing after the caveman. Finally, the caveman couldn't keep his footing on the

newly slick surface. He sailed across the rink, slamming into the railing on the other side. Shaggy managed to free himself from the blanket and threw it over the caveman just in time.

Chapter 9

Raye and Betty came running down through the seats to the rink.

"We saw everything from G. T.'s luxury box," Betty said. "I can't believe you actually caught him!"

"And now it's time to see who this caveman really is," Daphne said.

Raye reached over and pulled off the caveman's mask.

"Phyllis!" Raye exclaimed.

"Just as we suspected," Velma said.

"How did you know?" asked Betty.

"Well, it wasn't easy," Fred said. "The first couple of clues we found pointed at different suspects."

"Suspects? You mean you had more than one?" asked Betty. "Like who?"

"Probably me, for one," G. T. Barrington said, coming over. "I know I've got a reputation for doing just about anything to get publicity. It must have crossed your mind that I would do all this as a publicity stunt."

"You're right, Mr. Barrington," Daphne agreed. "You were our first suspect. The first clue we found matched something you're wearing."

"The caveman left a trail of wet boot prints behind," Velma said. "And you were the first person we met who was wearing boots."

"Who was the second?" asked Raye.

"Phyllis," Fred continued.

"But our second clue suggested that Joe Kresgee was involved," Daphne said.

"How could Joe be a suspect? He isn't even here," Betty said.

"I forgot to tell you, Betty," Raye said. "He stopped by earlier to see you. He was very upset."

"And he was wearing a red sweater that matched a red thread I found after the caveman chased Shaggy and Scooby," Velma said.

"But both of these clues also pointed to Phyllis," Fred said. "She was wearing work boots and a red muffler. It wasn't until the caveman locked us in the freezer that we found the last clue. A key."

"What kind of key?" Raye asked.

"The key that Scooby-Doo just used to help capture the caveman," Daphne said. "The key to the Zamboni machine."

"Once we found that key, we realized that whoever was behind this must have dropped it by accident," Velma explained. "That's how we got locked in the freezer. The caveman came back to find the key, but instead he found us."

"So that explains how the caveman disappeared after he took the skates," Raye said. "After he ran out onto the ice, he hid in the Zamboni closet."

"Which is where you'll find your silver skates, Betty," Daphne said.

"After all I went through to get you this job, Phyl, how could you do something like this?" asked Raye.

"I was tired of being everyone's gofer," complained Phyllis. "I wanted to prove that I have what it takes to be a professional skater. I didn't want to hurt anybody, I only wanted a chance to skate. I knew you'd never let me do it if I asked, so I created the whole caveman thing. I got the idea when G. T. told me to meet the ice truck. Once I put the phony caveman in there, everything else fell into place. And I would have gotten away with it and had my big break if it weren't for those kids and their meddling dog."

"Speaking of our meddling dog, has anyone seen Scooby?" asked Daphne. Just as she spoke, Scooby-Doo came gliding out of the Zamboni closet. Betty's silver skates were slung over his shoulder.

"Thanks, kids, I'm really grateful for your help," Betty said. "How can I ever thank you?"

"You don't have to thank us," Daphne said.

"I have an idea," Raye said.

That night, the gang had front-row seats for "Betty Kunkle's Silver Skates Arctic Ice Revue." Just before the intermission, Shaggy and Scooby got up to get some more hot cocoa. Then Betty invited Daphne, Fred, and Velma to join her on the ice. As they carefully stepped onto the ice to join Betty, the Zamboni machine burst through the green doors of its closet and out onto the ice. Shaggy drove as Scooby waved to the crowd.

Everyone burst into laughter and applause as Scooby called out to the crowd, "Scooby-Dooby-Doo!"

About the Author

As a boy, James Gelsey used to run home from school to watch the Scooby-Doo cartoons on television (only after finishing his homework). Today, he still enjoys watching them with his wife and two daughters. He also has a real dog named Scooby who loves nothing more than a good Scooby Snack!

Solve a Mystery With Scooby-Doo!

CARTOON NETWORK

SCOOBY DOO! MYSTERIES

by James Gelsey

Ruh-roh!

Zoinks!

READ THEM ALL!

$3.99 EACH!

❑ BDE 0-590-81909-7   #1: SCOOBY-DOO AND THE HAUNTED CASTLE
❑ BDE 0-590-81910-0   #2: SCOOBY-DOO AND THE MUMMY'S CURSE
❑ BDE 0-590-81914-3   #3: SCOOBY-DOO AND THE SNOW MONSTER
❑ BDE 0-590-81917-8   #4: SCOOBY-DOO AND THE SUNKEN SHIP
❑ BDE 0-439-08095-9   #5: SCOOBY-DOO AND THE HOWLING WOLFMAN
❑ BDE 0-439-08278-1   #6: SCOOBY-DOO AND THE VAMPIRE'S REVENGE
❑ BDE 0-439-11346-6   #7: SCOOBY-DOO AND THE CARNIVAL CREEPER
❑ BDE 0-439-11347-4   #8: SCOOBY-DOO AND THE GROOVY GHOST
❑ BDE 0-439-11348-2   #9: SCOOBY-DOO AND THE ZOMBIE'S TREASURE
❑ BDE 0-439-11349-0   #10: SCOOBY-DOO AND THE SPOOKY STRIKEOUT
❑ BDE 0-439-10664-8   #11: SCOOBY-DOO AND THE FAIRGROUND PHANTOM
❑ BDE 0-439-18876-8   #12: SCOOBY-DOO AND THE FRANKENSTEIN MONSTER
❑ BDE 0-439-18877-6   #13: SCOOBY-DOO AND THE RUNAWAY ROBOT
❑ BDE 0-439-18878-4   #14: SCOOBY-DOO AND THE MASKED MAGICIAN
❑ BDE 0-439-18879-2   #15: SCOOBY-DOO AND THE PHONY FORTUNE-TELLER
❑ BDE 0-439-18880-6   #16: SCOOBY-DOO AND THE TOY STORE TERROR
❑ BDE 0-439-18881-4   #17: SCOOBY-DOO AND THE FARMYARD FRIGHT
❑ BDE 0-439-24238-X   #18: SCOOBY-DOO AND THE CAVEMAN CAPER

At bookstores everywhere!

SCHOLASTIC. P.O. BOX 7502, JEFFERSON CITY, MO 65102

PLEASE SEND ME THE BOOKS I HAVE CHECKED ABOVE. I AM ENCLOSING $_____ (PLEASE COVER
SHIPPING AND HANDLING). SEND CHECK OR MONEY ORDER—NO CASH OR C.O.D'S PLEASE.

NAME_____ BIRTH DATE_____

ADDRESS_____

CITY_____ STATE/ZIP_____

PLEASE ALLOW FOUR TO SIX WEEKS FOR DELIVERY. OFFER GOOD IN USA ONLY. SORRY, MAIL ORDERS ARE
NOT AVAILABLE TO RESIDENTS OF CANADA. PRICES SUBJECT TO CHANGE.

SCOOBY-DOO AND ALL RELATED CHARACTERS AND ELEMENTS ARE TRADEMARKS OF HANNA-BARBERA © 2001.

CARTOON NETWORK AND LOGO ARE TRADEMARKS OF CARTOON NETWORK © 2001.